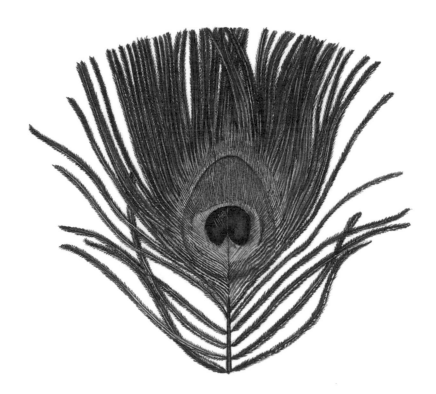

Beauty
and the
Beast

retold and illustrated by
JAN BRETT

CLARION BOOKS · NEW YORK

To Sarinda

ACKNOWLEDGMENT

When she was preparing this retelling of *Beauty and the Beast*, the author read a number of other versions of the story and found the one by Sir Arthur Quiller-Couch, published originally in 1910 by Hodder and Stoughton, London, to be especially helpful.

Illustration backgrounds airbrushed by Joseph Hearne.

Clarion Books
a Houghton Mifflin Company imprint
215 Park Avenue South, New York, NY 10003
Text and Illustrations copyright © 1989 Jan Brett Studio, Inc.

Library of Congress Cataloging-in-Publication Data
Brett, Jan, 1949-
Beauty and the beast / retold and illustrated by Jan Brett,
p.   cm.
Summary: Through her great capacity to love, a kind and beautiful
maid releases a handsome prince from the spell which has made him an
ugly beast.
PA ISBN 0-395-55702-X   ISBN 0-89919-497-4
[1. Fairy tales.   2. Folklore—France.]   I. Beauty and the beast.
II. Title.
PZ8.B675Be 1989   88-16965
398.2'1'0944—dc19   CIP
AC

HOR 10 9 8 7

nce upon a time, there lived a merchant's daughter so lovely and kind that all who knew her called her Beauty.

She lived with her father and two sisters in wealth and without worry. Then the merchant met with great losses and the family, suddenly penniless, fled to a country cottage. The man and his children were forced to do the work of peasants. Two of the sisters could only remember their former fine life, and cried and grumbled. But Beauty worked on bravely, and tried to comfort her father.

Time passed, until one day news came that one of the merchant's ships, long lost, had arrived in port. Hoping to restore his fortune, the merchant decided to meet the ship. Before leaving he called his three daughters to him. He asked them what they missed most from their old life, as he wanted to bring back a present for each.

The first sister asked for rich gowns, since her closet now held only rags. The second asked for a coach and four horses, since she was now forced to ride upon a donkey. But Beauty asked only for a rose, since the garden was now taken up with cabbages.

Upon reaching the ship, the merchant found the cargo spoiled and worthless. Poorer than ever, he could not afford a night's lodging, and was forced to return home through threatening weather.

He pushed through a deep forest until snow covered the track and he was hopelessly lost. Just when he felt he could no longer go on, he saw an avenue of orange trees, untouched by the snow, and beyond them a grand palace.

As the merchant approached the palace the doors opened up before him.
Inside he found himself in a great hall, with a blazing fire and a sumptuous
meal waiting. Strangely, he saw no one about. He dined, and soon fell asleep
in his chair.

The next morning the merchant awoke to find his wet clothes replaced
with fine garments. Again he saw no one, not master, or servant, or any per-
son in the house. When he stepped outside to go home, he met another kind-
ness. A magnificent horse, fitted out for a journey, stood waiting for him.

Just as he was about to mount the animal and be on his way, the merchant spied a bed of beautiful roses. Remembering his promise to Beauty, he knelt to pluck one.

No sooner had the stem snapped than the merchant heard a dreadful, angry roar. Turning around he saw a fearsome beast coming toward him. "How dare you harm my roses?" bellowed the Beast. "A rose that's cut can only die."

Reaching for his sword, the Beast cried, "You shall pay for your ingratitude with your life!"

The terrified merchant fell to his knees. "I have taken this rose only as a gift for one of my daughters, the faithful Beauty," he pleaded.

Hearing this, the Beast stopped to reconsider. At last he growled, "I will spare your life, but only if one of your daughters willingly returns in your stead."

The merchant was unable to agree to such a bargain. After promising the Beast that he would return, he rode home to say good-bye to his children.

It was a somber homecoming, for after the merchant gave Beauty the rose, he told the story of the grim Beast and his cruel punishment. But Beauty would not hear of her father's return to the palace and certain death. After all, he would never have plucked the rose if it weren't for her. She made up her mind to go at once in his place. And so strong was her resolve that the merchant could not dissuade her.

When father and daughter arrived at the palace of the Beast, the towering doors again opened as if by magic. They entered the great, empty hall and fear took hold of them. They heard the sound of footfalls and saw a creature, part man, part animal of the forest, move toward them.

Overcoming her terror, Beauty stepped forward. "Good evening my lord," she said.

"Good evening," replied the creature. "But do not call me 'my lord,' for I am a Beast, and you must call me so."

Not knowing what else to do, Beauty nodded. Then the Beast presented the merchant with a casket containing a fortune in coin and jewels. "This will restore your house handsomely," he said, "so now be gone." And with that the Beast walked off into the shadows.

The merchant bade a tearful farewell to Beauty. Then the great doors opened once more, and he rode away, leaving Beauty quite alone.

Thus Beauty began her new life in the palace of the Beast. It soon became clear that she was in no danger, and that she was free to amuse herself in any way she wished. She wandered among the rooms and explored the galleries. Each provided a delightful new entertainment for her, as if her tastes were already known.

A troop of monkeys all in court dress appeared to serve her. A charming little dog did duty as her page. In fact, animals of all sorts took the place of gardener, cook, and gamesman. A beautiful bird led her to her bedchamber, and Beauty saw that the room was filled with her favorite things and was thoroughly comfortable.

As evening approached, candles throughout the house lit up by them-
selves. When dinner was served animal musicians played sweet music. It was
then that the Beast appeared. Beauty drew back, frightened at the thought of
dining with the creature, but the Beast's courtly manners disarmed her fears.

After dinner the Beast reassured Beauty with charming conversation until it grew late. Then the Beast became solemn. At last he turned to her and
said, "Beauty, will you marry me?"

Beauty, lowering her eyes, replied, "Pray, don't ask me that."

The days afterward followed much the same pattern, and they passed happily for Beauty. The daylight hours were filled with amusements. And Beauty started to look forward to dinner-time and her nightly talks with the Beast. His thoughtful ways began to win her trust. But always she dreaded

the moment when he took his leave. For then he would always ask, "Beauty, will you marry me?"

It grew more and more painful for her to lower her eyes and say, "Pray don't ask me."

Then came a day that passed so happily that when the Beast came to her, Beauty spoke of her great joy. "The flowers in the gardens have never been more beautiful," she said. "And the musicians have never played more sweetly."

The Beast again asked for her hand, and with such tender hope that she
said, "I cannot marry you, Beast. But I will indeed stay here of my own accord
as long as I shall live, if only you will grant me one request. Let me first say
good-bye to my father and the world I leave behind."

The Beast agreed to this, although a mournful look came over him. He gestured to the crescent moon and said, "Return before the moon is full, faithful Beauty, or you will break your poor Beast's heart." Then he gave her a golden ring and said, "When you wish to come back, turn this ring three times around your finger and say aloud, 'I want to be in the palace of the Beast again.'"

Within the instant, Beauty was back in the house of her childhood. She saw her father bartering for goods as of old. Her sisters were ordering their maids about as in former times. Finding Beauty in their midst, they all flew to her in amazement. They asked question after question about her strange life in the palace, and about the monster who ruled there.

Beauty tried to explain her admiration for the Beast and the wonders of the palace, but they did not understand. They seemed pleased when the conversation flowed back to the social life of the town.

The following weeks went by in a whirl. Laughing young men coaxed Beauty to go out for walks or rides. Her father escorted her to concerts and the opera. And her sisters presented her with a list of engagements that began with dress fittings and ended with fancy balls. There was not a moment left in the day for her to think of the distant palace and the sad, ugly Beast. Beauty forgot her promise to him.

One night, after much gaiety and dancing, Beauty was exhausted. She fell into a fitful sleep, and as she slept she dreamed. She was back in the palace garden, now strangely dark and cold. She was searching and searching, looking for something she had lost. Then she saw the Beast lying on the ground, still as death.

Beauty awoke from the dream stricken with grief, but at last knowing her own heart. None of the young men she had met, none of the things she had done, meant as much to her as the times she had shared with the Beast.

Beauty turned the golden ring three times around her finger and said aloud, "I want to be at the palace of the Beast!"

At once she was transported through the night to the palace gates.
Guided by her dream, she flung them open and ran into the garden. There
she saw the still form of her beloved Beast.

26

Fearing that he might already have left this world, Beauty dropped to his side. And taking the Beast in her arms, she gave way to her sorrow. Her tears, raining down upon his furry head, worked to revive him, and he was able to open his eyes and look at her. At this she implored him, "Dearest Beast, you must be strong and live so that we may be man and wife, for I love you so."

When these words were spoken the world began to whirl around them.
Stars fell from the sky, and the palace was illuminated as if by a thousand
candles.

28

Before her Beauty saw not the Beast but the radiant face of a handsome young prince. For in pledging herself to the Beast, Beauty had unlocked a fantastic spell.

Taking Beauty's hand, the young prince explained all of the curious events to her. Some years before, a meddlesome fairy, displeased with people for trusting too much in appearances, had cast a spell over the palace and everyone in it. All of the servants were changed into animals, and the prince

was made to look like the ugliest and most fearsome Beast in the forest. The
spell would only be broken when a beautiful woman forsook all others and
promised to marry the Beast in spite of his appearance. And that is what
Beauty had done.

There was much rejoicing within the palace that night, but no one was happier than Beauty and the Prince. They were married the very next day, and went on to live happily ever after.

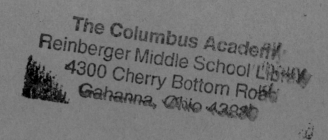